This Book Belongs To:

....

The Twelve Days of Christmas

This edition published by Parragon Books Ltd in 2017 and distributed by

Parragon Inc.
440 Park Avenue South, 13th Floor
New York, NY 10016
www.parragon.com

Illustrated by Caroline Pedler

ISBN 978-1-4748-9977-2
Printed in China

The
Twelve Days
of Christmas

PaRragon

Bath • New York • Cologne • Melbourne • Delhi
Hong Kong • Shenzhen • Singapore

On the first day of Christmas
my true love gave to me
a partridge in a pear tree.

On the second day of Christmas
my true love gave to me
two turtle doves
and a partridge in a pear tree.

On the third day of Christmas
my true love gave to me
three French hens,
two turtle doves
and a partridge in a pear tree.

On the fourth day of Christmas
my true love gave to me
four calling birds,
three French hens,
two turtle doves
and a partridge in a pear tree.

On the fifth day of Christmas
my true love gave to me
five gold rings,
four calling birds,
three French hens,
two turtle doves
and a partridge in a pear tree.

On the sixth day of Christmas
my true love gave to me
six geese a-laying,
five gold rings,
four calling birds,
three French hens,
two turtle doves
and a partridge in a pear tree.

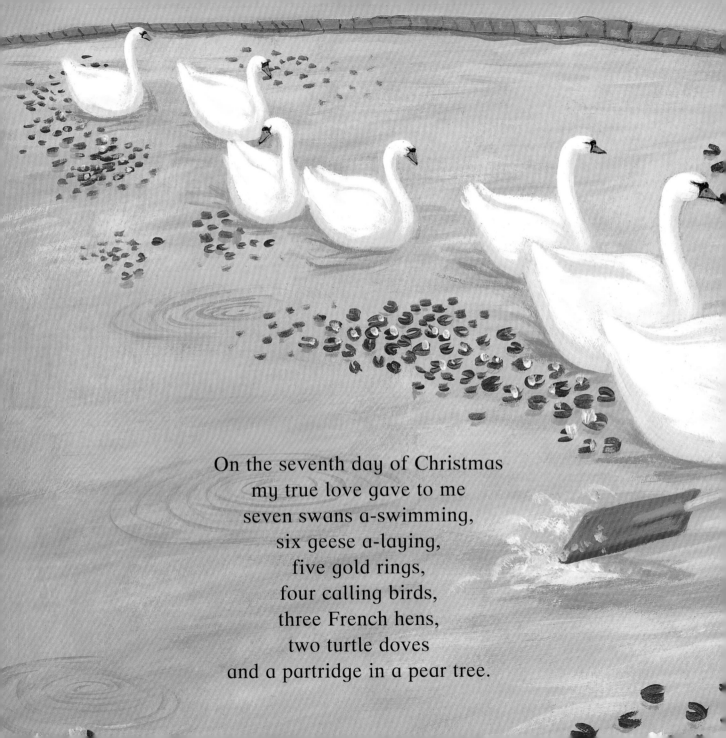

On the seventh day of Christmas
my true love gave to me
seven swans a-swimming,
six geese a-laying,
five gold rings,
four calling birds,
three French hens,
two turtle doves
and a partridge in a pear tree.

On the eighth day of Christmas
my true love gave to me
eight maids a-milking,
seven swans a-swimming,
six geese a-laying,
five gold rings,
four calling birds,
three French hens,
two turtle doves
and a partridge in a pear tree.

On the ninth day of Christmas
my true love gave to me
nine ladies dancing,
eight maids a-milking,
seven swans a-swimming,
six geese a-laying,
five gold rings,
four calling birds,
three French hens,
two turtle doves
and a partridge in a pear tree.

On the tenth day of Christmas
my true love gave to me
ten lords a-leaping,
nine ladies dancing,
eight maids a-milking,
seven swans a-swimming,
six geese a-laying,
five gold rings,
four calling birds,
three French hens,
two turtle doves
and a partridge
in a pear tree.

On the eleventh day of Christmas
my true love gave to me
eleven pipers piping,
ten lords a-leaping,
nine ladies dancing,
eight maids a-milking,
seven swans a-swimming,
six geese a-laying,
five gold rings,
four calling birds,
three French hens,
two turtle doves
and a partridge
in a pear tree.

On the twelfth day of
Christmas
my true love gave to me
twelve drummers drumming,
eleven pipers piping,
ten lords a-leaping,
nine ladies dancing,
eight maids a-milking,
seven swans a-swimming,
six geese a-laying,
five gold rings,
four calling birds,
three French hens,
two turtle doves
and a partridge
in a pear tree.

Complete Your
Christmas Treasury